3

The Hour of Separation

The Hour
of
Separation

A Love Story in Letters

J. M. Dallman

AONIAN PRESS
JAMES A. ROCK & COMPANY, PUBLISHERS
FLORENCE • SOUTH CAROLINA

The Hour of Separation: A Love Story in Letters by J. M. Dallman

is an imprint of JAMES A. ROCK & CO., PUBLISHERS

The Hour of Separation: A Love Story in Letters
copyright ©2011 by J. M. Dallman

Special contents of this edition copyright ©2011
by James A. Rock & Co., Publishers

Cover Photo: Nick Gleis Photography

Interior layout and design: Lynne Rock

Address comments and inquiries to:
AONIAN PRESS
James A. Rock & Company, Publishers
900 South Irby Street, #508
Florence, SC 29501
E-mail:
jrock@rockpublishing.com   lrock@rockpublishing.com
Internet URL: www.rockpublishing.com

ISBN/EAN: 978-1-59663-663-7

Library of Congress Control Number: 2008920489

Printed in the United States of America

First Edition: 2011

Ever has it been that love knows not its own depth
until the hour of separation.

— Kahlil Gibran

Is that you, Abelard?

It is I, Heloise!

Heloise!

Is that really you? My god — where are you?

What a wonderful surprise!

Heloise!

Dear Friend,

If that is really you — please prove it to me somehow. You know how deceptive this medium can be …

But I do so want it to be you!

It must be over twenty years now since we last spoke!

Or was it 'just an hour or so' ago …

My hands are trembling at the very thought of writing you, so I'll just press Send …

Heloise,

Yes, it is your old friend. For proof, I listened to Dinah Washington the other night over a bottle (or two) of wine and, of course, thought of you. It was the first time I'd listened to her in years — and I wept — yes, wept — at the mere memory of you. My heart even continued to pound late into the night destroying any possibility of sleep. And now here you are writing me not three days later — as if all those songs had actually summoned you up somehow!

Amazing.

I've often wondered over the years what happened to you …

In fact, it's been precisely twenty-two years, four months, one week and one day since we last met (although add another day to that equation should you decide to check your e-mail after midnight tonight).

Please tell me that you are happy and safe! And where the hell are you, by the way! Nearby or far? I've often thought about you with real affection — but, yes, also with real regret …

    Your Abelard

Dear Abelard,

I simply searched for your name and the words History Professor — and there you were.

Who knew it could be so easy? Twenty-two years? No problem. Just type away and press Send and wait a moment or two.

Wonderful!

Frightening …

Speaking of regrets, My Dear Abelard, why did we ever part … ?

    Your Heloise

Heloise,

First, I'm so pleased and delighted to be 'speaking' with you again. In fact, I feel a real sense of joy about it all. It's like a small miracle …

Why did we ever part? Because you moved to Paris to attend graduate school, of course, and that was the last time the two of us breathed the same air together … Of course you did invite me overseas to visit once or twice, but I was unable to go as I recall. Perhaps I should have made the effort, after all …

But do tell me all about you! Are you married now? Children? I know you've been writing some very interesting books over the years for I've followed your career quite closely. Well done, I must say! I would have expected no less from my star pupil.

Please tell me everything — and do not delay.

    Your Abelard

Dear Abelard,

Surely you could have contacted me over the years through my publisher somehow …

Is there a reason you did not … ?

As for my work, you should know right away that it was you — and you alone — who gave me the courage and confidence to even pursue such a career.

The pride you instilled in me in those early years transformed me. When I was too young and foolish to believe in myself — you showed me how. You respected my talent and insisted that we celebrate it. Yes, it was your simple but profound belief in me that changed me forever.

Thank you for that.

In fact, Sweet Abelard, in my youth — you were Everything to me.

You were my beacon, my inspiration, my wise man, my oracle, my source of happiness, my reason for living, my confidante, my protector, my brother, my partner in crime, my best friend, and my lover.

But, most of all, as the real Heloise often wrote to her own Abelard — you were my Only Love.

  Heloise

Heloise,

Please don't misunderstand me. You see, I mean no harm.

Of course I'm very excited to be conversing with you here again in this mysterious place — but there is something I must tell you right away. I am currently married — and even have two wonderful sons. Twins! Can you imagine — at my age? The boys just turned two years old in January — and are already quite good company — believe it or not.

My wife is a professor in the law department here, although she's recently decided to stay home full time with the twins. You'd like each other, I think. Perhaps you'd even like to visit us sometime. You'd be most welcome.

So, yes — as you can see — I did finally leave Her — perhaps two or three years after you left the country. I'm not sure what ultimately gave me the courage to do so. But are you ready for this? Within one lousy year she had remarried again! Can you imagine? All those guilt-filled years of feeling so duty-bound to her — feeling so indispensable to her happiness — yet wanting only you — all completely unnecessary!

As for my work, I've been quite nomadic since we last spoke, teaching and writing here and there, definitely on the move much like Abelard was in his day, although my restlessness has been more the result of boredom rather than professional jealousy. I currently head up the department here, and we have a good group of scholars assembled to teach a fine group of students. Strangely enough, I've found the sterling reputation of this place to be quite well deserved for a change. So I suppose that's the good news.

On the other hand, even challenging lectures and sophisticated class discussions do not put much money into the bank account. Nor do books on the Middle Ages sell all that well, to say the least. So I continue to remain financially strapped as usual — particularly considering the fact that I now have a young family to support for many years to come.

Ah, life. But others, I'm sure, have it far more difficult than I ...

But what about you, Sweet Heloise?

Please tell me all about yourself this very day!

Your Abelard

Thank you for not using my real name.

Nor will I ever allow you to use it again.

Nor will I ever say — or write — your name again.

Do you actually think that I'm going to titter, "How lovely — a new wife and two sons!"

Have you gone mad?

Have you forgotten the promise we made to each other!

Let us forget the formalities here.

You have betrayed me deeply — deeply — deeply — forever.

Heloise,

My god — you sound so angry with me.

Please don't be.

Of course I remember the promise we made to each other — but that was over two decades ago! We vowed to never, ever marry another — and even then to avoid marriage at all costs no matter what the situation. To us a marriage certificate was nothing more than a desperate attempt at ownership — you must remember that. It was yet another issue we both agreed upon completely.

So of course I remember our promise. I remember everything about you — I wish I didn't! If the truth be known your brilliance and beauty and grace have continued to haunt me since the very first day I laid eyes on you …

But how could either of us keep such a promise made in the flush of youth? How could we! Please answer me that!

And please don't be angry with me.

I will always have such very deep feelings for you.

    Your Abelard

Save your feelings for your new wife and sons.

Tell me only the facts — you who are so good at placing facts into their proper context.

Put your talents on display now — and tell me why you didn't go looking for me just as soon as you were set free — as you always promised to do.

Do you realize how many long years I waited in vain for you to leave her?

And do you realize how many more years after that I suffered in agony just thinking about you.

Yes, I turned to such things as my work and men and friends and travel — but all to no avail.

Instead I remained enslaved to the memory of your warm mouth on mine — enslaved to the memory of your brilliant lectures and books — enslaved to the memory of your soft hand holding mine as you carefully read my work …

And now you have married another — and had two children with her — when I was just a phone call away!

You counseled me over and over again to never marry. You said to keep myself free from such worldly constraints in order to pursue my all-important work — and I trusted and listened to your advice.

Yet now I am all alone while you write me proudly of your new family.

You have betrayed me just as cruelly as the real Abelard betrayed his own Heloise who wanted only to love and serve him — just as I wanted only to love and serve you.

Don't you see — purple prose or not — I would have clawed my way over the world's tallest mountain range in order to reach you.

I would have drained the very oceans of this earth in order to keep you safe.

I would have prevented this very planet from spinning in its orbit if it meant you'd be all mine.

And yet you couldn't make a single telephone call to me.

Instead you chose to imprison me — for life — in the convent of my career.

Such transparent rants disguised as good counsel!

Oh, yes — you have broken my heart yet again.

You have betrayed me yet again.

You have chosen another woman over me yet again.

But this time I will never, ever forgive you for it.

For now you have truly ripped my soul apart.

It lies in bloody pieces at my feet.

Heloise,

You mustn't say such things. You really mustn't. My heart will literally burst right open in grief and I'll quickly bleed to death right here at your feet. Your words have made me cry real tears of regret and shame. Please don't hate me! I'm so sorry to have hurt you once again.

Yes — maybe you're right — maybe I should have tried to find you just as soon as I became free. And maybe I should have continued to look for you until the very day I died. And maybe still — even today — I love you more than any other creature alive. Yes — maybe I do!

But how could I know that after so many years? How could I know that, My Darling? I couldn't know. So you must forgive me.

I did consider looking for you — I truly did. But then I grew afraid ...
Afraid you were happily married. Afraid you had found a rich man. Afraid
you had children without me. Afraid you had forgotten all about me. Afraid
you would be ill — or in trouble — or even dead! Afraid you were better off
without me. Afraid you'd be impossible to find again. Afraid you'd think I
was an old man. Afraid you'd notice my big gut and thinning hair. Afraid
you'd be bored with me suddenly. Afraid you'd be disappointed with my very
best books and lectures. Afraid you'd be smarter than I am now in my very
own field. Afraid I'd want to possess every inch of you all over again. Afraid
you had never loved me to begin with. Afraid you had stopped loving me
altogether. Afraid you would stop loving me one day in the future!

Heloise, please ... don't leave me just yet. ... I so desperately want to
connect with you at this time ...

Perhaps you could forgive me for just a little while — so that we could be
together — at least briefly — right here in this place. And we could talk
privately — as Abelard once wrote, saying things in letters that we'd never
have the courage to say in person ...

Please don't shut me out just yet.

I've only just found you again.

Icco, icco ... I beg you ... forgive me.

    Your Abelard

It was you who shut me out of your life — not the reverse.

And for what reason — I still don't know.

*And it was Heloise who used icco so often — while begging in vain for
Abelard's love — just as I've always begged for yours.*

Don't you see that my love for you has always transcended time — and distance — and space.

Not even death would have prevented me from finding you again.

Yet now it is too late.

You have rejected all that I have so freely and generously offered you.

Instead you have preferred me to be miserable and alone.

What kind of love is that!

I always gave you every last piece of myself so happily and generously.

And I would have done so again.

Yet you didn't care at all about the precious gifts I had to offer you.

Yes — Heloise's Only Love who destroyed her.

Just as my Only Love has destroyed me.

Can you honestly say that you love your wife more than you do me.

Can you honestly say that!

Oh, yes — you're living 'the good life' all right.

But just try hiding all the sadness you feel — you will fail.

You are a monster sent from hell to torment me.

Heloise,

My god … what have I done … No, I cannot say that … for maybe I do love you more than my very own wife. Maybe I do! In fact — maybe I love you more than life itself — it is true. But don't you see — there isn't a single thing I can do about that now!

Yes, indeed — our love is eternal — easily — but how could I know that back then! You were just a young girl barely out of her teens — and I was just a brand new college professor all love-soaked and guilt-ridden about wanting to worship his wonderfully sweet, loyal, and oh so brilliant student.

And No No No — I have never wanted you to be miserable and alone. On the contrary. That I can promise you, My Darling!

But what good are any of these confessions to us now? People are weak — and they often make mistakes — and life can be unfair as well. Why don't we just look ahead — and grasp at any little chance of happiness we might have right now — before we're both lost to each other forever.

Please, please … forgive me before it's too late …

    Your Abelard

P.S. Just as our love is timeless and profound — shouldn't it also be unconditional?

Do not blame this on life.

You did this to us.

You.

You.

No one else.

To Quote H: 'I wish I could think of some explanation which would excuse you and cover up the way you hold me so cheap.'

You know I have always fallen upon the scraps you've thrown me as if they were a feast.

And I was completely satisfied with them — because they came from the plate and the table of the very man I wished to devour.

But now you have left me to starve all alone — while the woman you chose over me feasts on the banquet that should have been all mine.

Yes, you have abandoned our great love for no reason at all.

You must never write to me again.

We are finished, My Cruel Darling.

Allow me to lick my wounds in peace.

You have proven to be My Worst Enemy.

My Darling Heloise,

Your words wound me deeply, to say the least …

You see, despite everything, I am still 'irresponsibly mad about you …'

But I've decided to simply ignore your anger for now and hope for the best.

Therefore, to 'make this moment sweet again,' I want to share with you some of my favorite memories of us together.

For example, I'll never forget the first day you walked into my class. I took one look at you — and my entire physical system all but shut down. The blood vessels in my head began to throb, my ears began to buzz very loudly, my poor heart lurched from side to side in my chest — and my legs — just moments before so sturdy and strong — began to tremble like a small child's. All this from just watching you walk across the room. Talk about enslaved at first sight. But I know I've told you that story many times before …

What I haven't told you is that you became my entire life that day. And I do not exaggerate. For years and years afterwards — only you mattered to me. Only your eyes and lips and arms and thoughts and opinions and smile meant anything at all to me. No one else even existed in my little world except for you and you alone …

Also, do you remember how we just stared at each other those first few weeks. How I wanted to kiss you — and put my hands and mouth all over you — everywhere — forgive me, but it's true. All I wanted to do was kiss your sweet body from top to bottom — morning to night — and then start kissing it all over again. I was filled with such an intense desire and longing for you that even my class lectures began to grow odd and disjointed from misguided emotion. And yet there you sat like an angel listening to every confused word I uttered. What a fool I made of myself over you. And what a fool I could make of myself again!

In short — the very first day I saw you — I was bewitched forever.

Please tell me you wish to hear more.

Your Abelard

P.S. You may remember Abelard's words on a similar subject:

'It was utterly boring for me to have to go to the school and equally wearisome to remain there and to spend my days on study when my nights were sleepless with lovemaking. As my interest and concentration flagged my lectures lacked all inspiration and were merely repetitive of what had been said before.'

P.P.S. You cannot accuse him of using too many commas.

My Dear Heloise,

I have waited one long week for a reply from you — yet have received nothing in return but silence. I suspect you're still very angry with me, which is entirely understandable, but please ... I beg you ... don't do this to me.

Instead let us return once again to our sweet past.

Even now I blush as I recall the first time we made love ... You may remember that day after class when you gave me a Dinah album with the song 'Teach Me Tonight' circled in red (yes, red) on the back. Needless to say, the boldness of your move threw me into an immediate and genuine lather — and I was so desperate to touch you by that time I even began to fear the physical evidence of my desire would make itself known in the classroom (which it did, as you know, that time I quickly hid behind the podium).

Then, just two days later, during my office hours, you suddenly strolled very nonchalantly into my office — wearing the prettiest summer dress I'd ever seen — and slowly closed the door behind you. You were seducing me! I became delirious with joy. I then locked the door behind you — took you into my arms — and pushed you up against the nearest wall ...

And then — Bliss. And Rapture. And Utter Joy. Yes — it was perhaps the happiest day of my entire life, if you can believe that.

After all, what can compare to making love to the one person you adore most in the whole world? Nothing ... nothing at all can compare.

Actually, what happened between us that day is beyond the power of words to describe. Not even the greatest poet could do it justice, so I won't even try. But that afternoon of love (yes — love) will remain with me until the very day I die.

And even now — as before — as Heloise would say — my desire for you knows no bounds.

Of course, you may recall that day altogether differently. But, to me, the touch of your curious hands traveling all over my body remains etched in my memory forever ...

Also, I recall another important detail from that day. Do you remember how perfectly silent we remained the entire time we made love? Yes — it was such a sacred event we even remained completely quiet somehow.

My god the things you could do to me.

And do to me still ...

You, alone — either before or since.

As Abelard, himself, once wrote:

> 'All on fire with desire for this girl I sought an opportunity of getting to know her through private daily meetings and so more easily winning her over ...'

Believe me — I wanted only to love you — never to hurt you.

Your Abelard

P.S. How do you remember that day?

My Sweet Heloise,

I await your response. Please don't keep me waiting any longer in this terrible state of sorrow and anxiety.

Meanwhile, again from Abelard, as if from our very own past:

'… and so with our lessons as a pretext we abandoned ourselves entirely to love. Her studies allowed us to withdraw in private, as love desired, and then with our books open before us, more words of love than of our reading passed between us, and more kissing than teaching. My hands strayed oftener to her bosom than to the pages; love drew our eyes to look on each other more than reading kept them on our texts.

'… In short, our desires left no stage of love-making untried, and if love could devise something new, we welcomed it. We entered on each joy the more eagerly for our previous inexperience, and were the less easily sated.'

I've always loved that particular passage of his. But please — do believe that my only motive — ever — was simply to get close to you.

Your Abelard

17

Dearest Friend,

Since my e-mails are not bouncing back, I will assume that you have read all my letters with some measure of recognition and pleasure.

It's been three weeks now since your last missive — and I remain highly impatient to hear from you again. Please don't punish me this way with your unhappy silence. Instead let us care for each other right here in this place — in whatever small way we can — before our short time together ends suddenly.

What H wrote on this very subject:

'I beg you then to listen to what I ask — you will see that it is a small favour which you can easily grant. While I am denied your presence, give me at least through your words — of which you have enough and to spare — some sweet semblance of yourself. It is no use my hoping for generosity in deeds if you are grudging in words …'

Also, it seems to me that we have skipped a few e-mails here. Shouldn't I have asserted my commitment to my marriage at least a few more times in these lines — and shouldn't you have painted a lovely picture of your life there full of lovers and friends and parties and speaking tours. But no — instead we have just skipped right over all that, haven't we, My Darling — only to plunge once again into the very depths of our love …

Just as before, when we are alone together, the outside world holds no interest for us whatsoever.

As George Eliot said:

'The first sense of mutual love excludes other feelings; it will have the soul all to itself.'

Yes …

I do love you, you know, Sweet Heloise. And I always will.

Your Abelard

Lovers seek willingly new roads; the married seek the old.
— *Russian Proverb*

What would your sweet wife have to say about such declarations of love to me?

You have a family to think about now.

It's far too late to even think about loving me.

Keats said, 'Love is my religion.'

And so it is mine.

But your religion is Security — and Certainty.

Or — put another way — I am a whore for Love — of which I am proud — while you are merely a whore for Safety.

> *No one worth possessing*
> *Can be quite possessed.*
> — *Sara Teasdale*

You choose only submissive, compliant women who will never leave you.

But how interesting is that bland brand of loyalty.

How clever and challenging is a woman like that really.

Answer me that right now.

Fool! Fool!

Only I know how to love you the way you truly deserve.

And only you know how to love me properly as well.

Why couldn't you see that!

You have ruined any hope of happiness for either of us — either alone or together.

> *Of all forms of caution, caution in love is perhaps the most fatal to true happiness.*
> *— Bertrand Russell*

Also, you quote Heloise. Allow me to do the same — although I will never, ever read or refer to their letters again.

> *'But if I lose you, what is left for me to hope for? What reason for continuing on life's pilgrimage, for which I have no support but you, and none in you save the knowledge that you are alive, now that I am forbidden all other pleasures in you and denied even the joy of your presence which from time to time could restore me to myself ...'*

How she suffered as I do now.

Cruel, cold Abelards.

> *'O Fortune who is only ill-fortune, who has already spent on me so many of the shafts she uses in her battle against mankind that she has none left with which to vent her anger on others. She has emptied a full quiver on me, so that henceforth no one else need fear her onslaughts ... Of all wretched women I am the most wretched, and amongst the unhappy I am unhappiest. The higher I was exalted when you preferred me to all other women, the greater my suffering over my own fall and yours, when I was flung down; for the higher the ascent, the heavier the fall ...'*

Yes, like my namesake, amongst the unhappy, I am the unhappiest ...

My Friend,

You use no name at either the top or bottom of your letters. This disturbs me greatly. And from Heloise — who so loved her salutations. You see, only now am I beginning to realize the true gravity of the situation here — so please be patient with me. And you must also try to find some measure of forgiveness for me rather quickly — even if only temporarily — for — once again — we may have so little time left here, as I've said repeatedly.

But let us look again to our past for comfort, shall we? Somehow it seems to help me.

And now about your fine kiss.

Ah — it was a kiss like no other! First, of course, it was soft and silky smooth — but also very needy and hungry — as if you were sucking the very marrow out of my bones with your sweet slippery tongue … as if you were exploring the very core of my being in big sexy wet gulps. Ah, that kiss … suffice to say that it was absolutely delicious and dangerous in every way. Yes — it was 'that voodoo that you do so well.' (There is still no one finer than Dinah … have you listened to her recently?)

Also, I'm finally beginning to understand what transpired now …

But believe me — if the truth be told — I'd rather spend just one hour with you than a lifetime with anyone else.

I'm reminded of a wonderful epigram about that if I can find it.

Yes, here it is:

> One hour of right-down love is worth an age of dully living on.
> — Aphra Behn

In fact, I'm remembering your warm mouth pressing against mine right now. Oh yes — I'm mad with desire for you all over again.

And yet, I have a life to live here as well … I have a family who needs me. Yet all I can think about is lying on top of you and pressing your bottom ever closer to mine …

Your Abelard

P.S. Do you remember how we cried sometimes when we made love? How odd that seems to me now — yet at the time it seemed so normal. Also, in my defense, regarding the above, remember: — the deeper my love — the deeper my desire …

H,

I have waited another long week to hear from you — but nothing — nothing at all. All those long hours of waiting were merely in vain. Damn your cruel silence. And damn your wish to punish me! But I've decided to write you anyway — for I've a very important observation to make.

Can you believe that we — of all people — are exchanging love letters!

(Or I am anyway!)

Could it have been otherwise?

How very odd, isn't it?

As Abelard wrote:

> 'Knowing the girl's knowledge and love of letters I thought she would be all the more ready to consent, and that even when separated we could enjoy each other's presence by exchange of written messages in which we could speak more openly than in person, and so need never lack the pleasures of conversation …'

Also — do you recall how we used to list our similarities to our favorite lovers? Here are the ones I can remember at the moment:

Somehow we were (and are) not of this century.

The Middle Ages — and French — connection

The academic connection

I am14 years older than you (one of the strangest coincidences of all)

You were my most brilliant student (by a country mile)

We became secret lovers

We, too, made love in the most public, dangerous places

Our affair was socially unacceptable

Most of all, we fell desperately — and forever — in love.

And now for the new similarities:

It was our work that led to our sad — no, tragic — separation

It was we Abelards who were — and are — to blame

And now, of course, we're exchanging love letters.

Perhaps the last coincidence is the strangest of all ...

On the other hand — I do see one very big difference between us.

The 12th century Heloise never gave up on her Abelard.

Please think about that very carefully ...

    Your A

You seem to have forgotten one other very important similarity.

H,

How good to finally hear from you! And yet you offer me only one lousy sentence? I don't remember you being so stingy with your words …

As for the last similarity … I thought we had promised each other to never speak of that sad event again. No, I hadn't forgotten about that at all … I was merely respecting your explicit wish to bury that memory forever …

On another subject, it occurred to me that we might have chosen a more cheerful, lucky pair of lovers to model ourselves after — to put it mildly.

I speak, among other things, of the terrible fate that awaited poor A. Earlier this evening I read a detailed account of a typical Middle Ages castration — a brutal operation that was done much the same way on both farm animals and men alike (adulterers usually). I won't go into detail here, but suffice to say that it involved the use of a simple cord and sharp knife.

I do hope you don't have a jealous uncle lurking around somewhere.

Your Abelard

P.S. Please write and include details of your current life. You have told me absolutely nothing so far.

Dear Heloise,

> 'Love makes the wildest spirit tame, and the tamest spirit wild.'
> — A. Delp

Now that quotation fits us exactly. Yes, it appears that only I could tame you — and only you could un-tame me . . .

But listen to me — I'm starting to get angry now — and simply must receive a letter from you very soon or I'll not continue to write. Do you hear me? It's just too painful to wait and wait for weeks on end — only to get nothing at all in return. In fact, it's downright brutal of you to ignore me like this. I know that you're receiving these letters — so please send me at least a few kind words before I lose my very sanity. Do you hear me!

And now here are more of my fondest memories, since reminiscing does seem to give me some semblance of relief. More importantly — maybe such tender recollections will even serve to win you over partially (please do take pity on me).

So pay close attention now because I'm going to recount all the wonderful places where we made love.

These are just the ones I can remember right now, however, and I'll include only the locations on campus. After all, the nights at your place — and on the road — are different e-mails altogether.

Oh, yes, we Made Love . . .

In my office, of course (my office hours have never been the same)

In the dark wings of the main theatre, buried deep in the black velvet drapes (perhaps my favorite place of all)

Backstage in the little theatre as well

In the library stacks (very dangerous — your idea, of course)

In various and assorted custodian closets

In various and assorted restrooms (I know, I know, but I'd do it all over again)

In the conference room on the fourth floor of the library
(remember how we would tape a piece of paper over the small window on the door?)

In the student lounge after hours (yes, we were that desperate)

In the faculty lounge after hours (your idea once again — a wonderful memory)

In the car (many, many times) at night

In the car during the day

Behind the science and art and music buildings at night

In the chapel loft that one time as the clock chimed midnight. (How could I forget that night. And remember how we loved climbing that lovely steep path to the church!)

In the art studios (where the smell of paint always made us high)

And in those tiny music rehearsal rooms (where we could be as loud as we wished).

Ah, yes ... good times indeed ...

As H once wrote, it appears my mind is 'still on fire with its old desires ...'

And yet our assignations back then were not without shame on my part, believe me. Where was my sense of decency, after all! But at least you remain — to this day — the only student I ever made love to. That much I can promise you.

Also, as I look back now, we never once got caught. But it was never about that, was it? No, instead it was just about holding each other as tightly as possible, for as long as possible … that was all.

But oh yes, we did find 'what the rest have left behind …'

(That's one of my favorite songs of hers, by the way.)

And please tell me what places I've forgotten!

From H:

> 'It is very difficult to tear the heart away from hankering after its dearest pleasures …'

And, again, from A:

> 'After our marriage, when you were living in the cloister with the nuns at Argenteuil and I came one day to visit you privately, you know what my uncontrollable desire did with you there, actually in a corner of the refectory, since we had nowhere else to go …'

> Your A

Heloise,

I must give you fair warning: I will not continue to write unless I receive some words of encouragement from you! I desperately need to connect with you at this time — even if in this distant and strange fashion. I'm terribly, terribly lonely for you now. Can't you see that!

Also, I've been meaning to tell you something … Surely it isn't too late for you to find another man to love deeply. You who have so much to offer a lover. Believe me, I know …

> Your Abelard

You have the audacity to tell me to love another man?

Has your very heart been removed from your chest and placed in another by chance?

I have been in agony since the very moment we began speaking again.

My tears are spilling everywhere — all over my cheeks and lips and chin and hands and arms and thighs — and then I look up to find deep red bruises under my eyes.

You gave me those bruises. You.

Sometimes I simply pull the car over just to sit and cry.

When I walk, I even lean forward now so the tears will fall directly to the ground instead of all over me.

And yet you encourage me to love another?

You are a cold, cruel, heartless man.

Heloise,

> Lips that taste of tears, they say are the best for kissing.
> — D. Parker

Thank you for your words, terribly sad though they were. But at least they were words. I am finding it increasingly difficult to realize I am the sole cause of your grief. The deep pain all this has stirred up inside me is both acute and alarming.

Indeed — what have I done to us? What have I done! I was free to go to you. Free to love and care for you alone! And yet I did nothing — nothing at all. Yes — I can understand why you hate me now. Where in the world was my courage when I needed it most? Only cowardice has kept me away from you all these years — just cowardice.

Can you ever forgive me? Can I ever forgive myself!

From my much wiser namesake:

> 'There is nothing worse than a foolish man blessed by fortune … I am paying the price for stupidity, because I am losing that good thing of which I have been completely unworthy, that good thing which I have not known how to keep as I ought. It is flying elsewhere, forsaking me, because it realizes that I am not worthy of having it.'

A

I have forgiven you several times before for the grievous errors you have committed against me.

And I did so with affection and tenderness.

I've also forgiven you for the lesser flaws in your character — flaws I even embraced as virtues because they belonged to the man I loved.

But how can I forgive this most extreme form of neglect and treachery.

Just like the real A — your brilliant mind is useless when it comes to affairs of the heart.

As H once told her own betrayer: 'I would have followed you into the very fires of hell.' It appears I have actually done so.

Heloise,

Yes, this is what she wrote:

> 'I would have had no hesitation, God knows, in following you or
> going ahead at your bidding to the flames of Hell. My heart was not
> in me but with you, and now, even more, if it is not with you it is
> nowhere; truly, without you it cannot exist.'

I, too, feel in the throes of some sort of hell. All the happiness I once found
in my family is now on hold — for I can think only of you. Please don't
keep me waiting any longer for your forgiveness ... even if it is temporary. I
won't let you down this time — I promise.

The following says it all.

> Sexual love is the most stupendous fact of the universe, and the
> most magical mystery our poor blind senses know.
> — Lowell

> Your Abelard

Heloise,

At least write and tell me that you despise me — but please write me
something — anything at all. Trust me, My Love: I'm suffering just as
deeply as you are — for I'm the sole cause of all this misery.

So let us return again to our happier past.

Forgive me if I write about your body again, but I cannot get it out of my
mind.

Yes, your lovely body was my favorite one of all. It was so small and soft and round (with the scent of talcum powder as I recall). Yet your arms and legs were so strong against mine, so hungry and unafraid, so happy and laughing, so slow yet so fast, so gentle yet so rough, so wonderfully in control — yet so out of control at the same time.

My god, what I want to do to you right now.

Once again … just an earth-shaking, foundation-rocking desire to possess you in every way I know how.

Your A

Listen to Bargain Day if you wish to know the current state of my body.

In the past it was your eyes and mouth and hands that gave me such joy before the downfall.

Now it is your paragraphs and words and commas that will make me crash and fall.

Just as you have spoiled me for all men in the future — so, too, have I spoiled you.

Good — I am glad for that.

It is only fair.

Heloise,

Ah, yes, Bargain Day. How we both loved her so (and still do to this day). No one understands a song the way she does (another matter we both agreed on completely). Of course you must remember performing her songs for me. Those memories, in particular, have served to haunt me. That day you sang 'Squeeze Me' while sitting on my lap just before a class I ... oh never mind ... but you sure could shake that little tail of yours all right ...

There was another song you sang to me as well — your favorite, I think: 'Nothing in the World.' In fact, it was that song that summoned you up somehow ... How well you always loved me. What in the world was I thinking!

On another subject ... I must tell you something else I remember with great pleasure. The scholarship of your work was phenomenal. Your papers always surpassed all current research on the subject with an agility and brilliance that left me quite speechless. At first I didn't even believe you'd written them, do you remember? But you had. You were that capable. I was genuinely intimidated by your intellect on a daily basis. You must recall me telling you that as well.

In fact — to this day I require every one of my students to read your paper titled 'Matriarchy in Castle Life.' Do you remember that one? It is still the finest example of creativity and scholarship on the undergraduate level I have ever seen. There was no pretense or ego in your writing at all — just brilliant, eccentric leaps and bounds that no one else could possibly make.

In fact, I think I've missed your intellect throughout the years even more than your heavenly body.

But back to Dinah ... I must say that you sounded damn good singing along with her — and you sure could dance as well.

Must go now. Work calls, I'm afraid.

Your Abelard

Heloise,

Sad and alone, I await word from you …

But meanwhile the memories keep coming back to me — sometimes suddenly in a great big rush (such as when I found your photographs again — oh my god! — what emotions! but more on that later). Or sometimes they come back to me very slowly after I close my eyes and simply try to see your face again …

For example, do you remember how we always liked to read that one particular translation of their letters? We cried every single time we read them. How sentimental we were. Yet their story remains just as sad to me today … perhaps more so … How lovers have suffered since the beginning of time.

And now here are more random memories that serve to keep me up at night …

* Do you remember the Halloween party we attended dressed as A & H? We had such fun dancing in those ridiculous costumes. You and I — stubborn atheists — pretending to be a monk and nun of all things. (I could find no costume for a 12th century logician, however.) Do you realize that was the first — and last — time I ever danced in my entire life?

* And you must remember the magic wand you sent me the first Christmas you were away. ('I'd wave it for no one but you'). Guess what? It's sitting on my desk at work this very minute.

* And do you remember your all-nighters when you would type furiously all night long while mumbling all sorts of strange things under your breath? I thought you were a bit mad back then, but now I see that it was sheer talent instead ...

* And one of my favorite memories of all! The first year you were away we always looked at the moon together at the same time every Sunday night — you must remember that. (The time difference always made me feel so lonely for you somehow.) Yes, I remember that so clearly. It always amazed me that we could look at the exact same moon — at the exact same time — yet still remain continents apart ...

* And I remember your hip bones, oddly enough, and the way they poked up in that big, round, curvy way when you rested on your side. You called them devil horns, I believe. They certainly brought out the devil in me ...

Well, I have many, many more memories if you're at all interested ...

A

My Distant Love,

Remember what H wrote when she finally became resigned to his indifference:

'For nothing is less under our control than the heart — having no power to command it we are forced to obey. And so when its impulses move us, none of us can stop their sudden promptings from easily breaking out, and even more easily overflowing into words ... I will therefore hold my hand from writing words which I cannot restrain my tongue from speaking; would that a grieving heart would be as ready to obey as a writer's hand!'

Not that my writer's hand will ever obey.

Please assure me that — unlike our namesakes — we will be together — at least briefly — someday.

    Abelard

My Friend in Both Life and Love,

> Love is of all the passions the strongest, for it attacks
> simultaneously the head, the heart, and the senses.
> — Voltaire

Now that is a fine quotation. Yes, love is the very point of life.

In a recent letter I mentioned famous lovers in history . . . Was it Tristen or Isolde who said that love is even greater than death? Yes, that is indeed true. Please do remember that . . .

And do you recall how Dante had to immediately lie down and rest simply because he caught a glimpse of his beloved Beatrice?

How vulnerable we human creatures are to love.

And do you remember what Catherine said about Heathcliffe:

> 'Whatever our souls are made of, his and mine are the same . . .'

Yes, we, too, are the same.

But why must great love always include such terrible suffering!

I'm so lonely for you tonight I cannot even sign my name.

Heloise,

> A pity beyond all telling
> Is hid in the heart of love.
> — W. B. Yeats

I await! Please tell me how I can reach you ...

I have been haunted by the memory of our last good bye ...

You must remember that terrible night. We were standing on the train station platform sobbing inconsolably in each other's arms. I think we both knew we'd be parting for a very long time ... I remember that my shirt collar was completely wet from your tears, and there were two children standing down the platform pointing and laughing at us because we were crying so hard ...

I wanted to end my very life that night when you left me behind ...

My very heart disappeared with you down that long, dark, train track ...

    A

Heloise,

It has been one month and one day since my last letter to you — and I will NOT write to you again. I really will not! It is simply too painful an undertaking for me. Apparently you have very little interest in either my current thoughts, or in the memories I hold so dear.

On the other hand, I have thought about you every single minute since the day you found me again. Why is that, I wonder? Why is it that you, and you alone, can reach the very core of my being? But I do refuse to send you even one more letter without a reasonable and timely response of some kind!

To quote my namesake yet again:

> 'Would you want to be partners only in joy, not grief, to join in rejoicing without weeping with those who weep? There is no wider distinction between two friends and false than the fact that the former share adversity, the latter only prosperity.'

Also, do you remember how they used to call each other Sun and Moon? That always touched me somehow.

A

A,

Your memories would be most welcome if only I could bear to remember them.

But words are cheap and easy to hide behind.

Where was your great love for me when you stood at the altar reciting your vows to your new wife?

And where was your great love for me when you took her into your arms night after night and gave her two beautiful sons!

But, yes … despite everything, I do still love you.

It is true.

Yet you have doomed us both to lives of great loneliness, great sorrow, and great regret.

I suffer for both of us equally.

H

Heloise,

Finally! Thank you for those kind words …

Did you know that I always re-read your e-mails over and over again, perhaps a hundred times or so?

Here is what A wrote about that.

> 'Indeed your words are few, but I made them many by re-reading them often. I do not measure how much you say, but rather how bountiful is the heart from which it comes.'

Also, I was remembering how you were always so kind and thoughtful to everyone — just like your mother was. Your sweet nature was always one of your greatest assets. Do you remember the boy with the terrible acne that you befriended one semester in my class? His face was transformed within a matter of months simply because of his friendship with you. Believe me, I saw it with my own eyes.

Also, My Darling, I'm not sure what it is you want from me right now …

Further apologies? More reasons why? More declarations of love? More memories?

Please tell me what would make you happy at this time! I promise to satisfy you if I possibly can. For just as you were always there to serve me — I wish now to serve only you.

Your Abelard

I simply want to know why.

I still don't understand why …

Heloise,

All right — let me try to explain further. When I was married the first time, I wrongly placed duty before love. I was a fool. Since there were no children involved, I should have left her immediately for you — no question about that (even if my professional reputation had suffered for it). But this time — with children in the picture — duty must take precedence over love. It can be no other way. You see, children need their fathers — particularly at this age — and so I must stay here to fulfill my obligations — there is no question about that.

You see, I simply cannot, and will not, leave my boys behind — not even for you. Yes, I could leave my wife to be with you — that much is true. I know I shouldn't admit such a thing aloud — nor write such a thing down — but it's true. I see now I'd leave any woman in the world behind to be with you! But I cannot — and will not — leave my sweet boys behind …

On the other hand — I must explain further — I do love my wife very much. Make no mistake about that. She's a good, clever, loving woman who has made me quite happy, in fact. But it appears that only you can truly transport me …

Does that answer your question at all?

Or are you asking why I failed to look for you? Again, fear. There was certainly no lack of love. I suppose that most of all I was afraid you'd tire of me one day — and leave me — a situation I couldn't bear to even contemplate, let alone tolerate. So in the end I was simply protecting myself above all, I suppose. Shamefully, that does appear to be my first priority, doesn't it?

On the other hand, if the truth be told, I also felt you deserved far better than me — an obscure historian with dry, scholarly books long out of print — and a bank account that could hardly pay for a trip overseas to visit you. So that's certainly another part of the equation ...

Or perhaps you're asking why I would marry again at all? To be perfectly honest, I don't know. I've always shuddered at the very idea of marriage (as did you) — and yet here I am. Perhaps it was simply good old fashioned love that led me down the aisle again. Or maybe it was a big dollop of boredom, or maybe it was just the need to belong to something other than a claustrophobic college community.

Or maybe I saw (and see) my wife as someone who would help me face the big bad world — cruel as it can sometimes be. I've heard that many men marry for that reason, for the emotional support they receive — and perhaps I'm just an ordinary mortal after all, just another sheep in the herd, looking for that very same thing despite all my foolish pride.

Dear Friend — does that begin to answer your questions at all?

Your Abelard

A,

There are more whys.

Please answer them all.

   Your H

Heloise,

Thank you for your final salutation. Are you still really mine — to this very day? How I wish to be yours in this strange, intimate place we've found!

There are more whys to be answered?

Should I enter forbidden territory … ?

   Your Abelard

Yes, if you dare …

Heloise,

Now you've frightened me somehow … I hesitate to bring up such a sad time in our lives. Must we really go back to that place? If there is anything to be learned or gained from it, then, yes, let's do so. But if not ….

Also, again on the subject of why I didn't call you, sometimes I wonder if just the simple act of having more money would have changed my behavior somehow. In other words, would even a little bit of wealth have given me the confidence I needed to pursue you? Sadly, I suspect so — which is yet another sad commentary on my questionable values I suppose …

Yes, perhaps I have become what I've always feared the most … just another struggling, average man on the street.

Whatever became of my plans to do great things!

    Your Abelard

Abelard,

    Who, being loved, is poor?
— O. Wilde

No, you are a wise, thinking man — the shepherd of the herd.

I've known that since the first time I saw you (and, yes, it was all as you described that day, for me as well).

But you have battered and abused this poor ewe in your care.

You have left it to roam the meadows all alone and unguarded, hungry and cold, in the darkest part of the night.

How lost I am now …

Heloise,

Thank you for your kind comment, though I hardly deserve it.

If the truth be known, my heart is so very heavy right now — for you, for me, for my wife, for my sons ...

We all seem to be missing something so important in our lives. I feel such a sense of dread — as if all of us are doomed to a life of great loneliness somehow ...

Please tell me all my fears are misguided.

And please tell me once again that you love me.

　　Your Abelard

Heloise,

Are you there?

Must I wait for you forever!

How I am suffering here.

Sweet Heloise,

I am now going to list The Three Reasons why I love you so much.

You are a Great Thinker.

You are a Great Talker.

You are a Great Listener.

Also, I can't seem to find the source of this quote, but it certainly seems to resonate with me now.

> True love cannot be found
> Where it truly does not exist,
> Nor can it be hidden where it truly does …

I remain afraid, My Darling, so afraid for us!

A

⌒⌒

Abelard,

> *Love and a cough cannot be hid.*
> *— English Proverb*

You're frightening me now … for I too feel a real sense of doom as if something were terribly wrong with our lives somehow.

I've also been thinking a great deal about my lengthy silences, and how much they've been punishing you …

Nor has my behavior led to the kind of answers I crave so badly, though you did, indeed, try to satisfy me.

So I am going to partially forgive you for now — but only for a little while. For in the near future we will be saying a final good bye.

We must. You know that.

This cannot go on indefinitely.

I would not survive it.

> *Your Heloise*

⌒⌒

H,

You mentioned that you're frightened of something … please explain
further.

    A

A,

*Maybe it's the simple fact that we belong together, but will never be
together.*

*Or maybe it's the fact that I agree with you so completely about your
boys.*

Of course you belong with them — always and forever.

*Or maybe my uneasiness comes from the fact I've been worrying about
your health of all things. Isn't that silly? I even had a dream last night
that you were castrated by a mob of your students for loving me and not
them! I know it's probably the Abelard connection — but the
coincidences do continue to mount, don't they? I just can't seem to shake
the feeling that you're at risk somehow …*

Have you, by any chance, seen a doctor recently?

I, myself, have lost ten pounds since our sad correspondence began.

I am literally starving to death here without you.

It seems that only you can provide the sort of sustenance I need.

Please don't let me waste away — not yet anyway …

    Your Heloise

H,

Please tell me where the hell you are living.

I need to know that at once. I suspect you're still in France — but am I right? At least tell me in what city you reside. This virtual world is disconcerting enough without a lot of unnecessary secrecy adding to the confusion.

Please … I need some sort of tangible place to hold onto right now …

This is important to me.

    A

A,

It doesn't matter where I live.

In the real world we are lost to each other forever.

We have only this tiny piece of space to share together now — and I suspect not even that for much longer.

I asked if you have seen a doctor recently, and you never answered me. I continue to worry about your health, although admittedly for no discernable reason.

    Your H

H,

I'm fine — please don't worry about me. But even back then you watched over me like a mother hen — remember? You did love me very, very deeply, didn't you? I was always certain of that …

Also, I thought of something else quite sad today. Do you realize that we have never lived under the same roof together!

How did we allow that to happen!

Ah — I would do it all so differently now!

 Your A

Abelard,

That remains my greatest wish to this day: to live with you — the only man I ever truly loved — under the same roof.

My greatest wish lost.

Baudelaire had it right:

 'Love is an oasis of horror in a desert of boredom.'

No, My Heloise!

 That love is all there is,
 Is all we know of love.
 — E. Dickinson

Love is only a dirty trick played on us
  to achieve the continuation of the species.
  — *W. S. Maugham*

No ...

  Love is never lost. If not reciprocated,
  it will flow back and soften and purify the heart.
  — W. Irving

Believe me, My Abelard:

  Scratch a lover, and find a foe.
  — *D. Parker*

No again!

  Love is all we have,
  the only way that each can help the other.
  — Euripides

Love is a wound that never heals.
— *German proverb*

Love is the greatest refreshment in life.
— Picasso

Wrong!

> *The pleasure loves gives is not*
> *really worth the happiness it destroys.*
> — *R. Hahn*

You know this much to be true!

> We are most alive when we're in love.
> — J. Updike

No, this is true:

> *There is no pain equal to that which*
> *two lovers can inflict on one another.*
> — *B. Connolly*

H,

Do you really believe that? Have you really lost all faith in romantic love? You who didn't have a cynical bone in your body!

My faith in eternal love has only been strengthened by our tender reunion.

Yes, it's been painful, but on the other hand:

> The great object of life is sensation —
> to feel that we exist, even in pain.
> — Lord Byron

Your Abelard

> *Love is the beginning of sorrow.*
> — *German proverb*

No …

> He whom love touches not walks in darkness.
> — Plato

Heloise,

I await. It's your turn to go now, you know.

But all right … I'll go again.

> To cheat oneself out of love is the most terrible deception;
> it is an eternal loss for which there is no reparation,
> either in time or eternity.
> — S. Kierkegaard

> *Love's pleasure lasts but a moment;*
> *Love's sorrow lasts all through life.*
> *— J. Claris de Florian*

My Darling,

No — I believe this:

> To love and win is the best thing.
> To love and lose, the next best.
> — W. M. Thackeray

> *He who loves the more is the inferior and must suffer.*
> *— T. Mann*

What a grand thing to be loved!
What a grander thing still, to love!
— V. Hugo

One seeks to make the loved one entirely happy, or,
if that cannot be, entirely wretched.
— J. de la Bruyere

Love, like virtue, is its own reward.
— M. I. Ezra

Love is the desire to prostitute oneself.
— C. Baudelaire

Love makes your soul crawl out of its hiding place.
— Z. N. Hurston

Heloise ... where are you ... I am waiting!

All right, I'll simply go again …

> Love is the only sane and satisfying
> answer to the problem of human existence.
> — E. Fromm

Sweet Heloise,

Please don't keep me waiting any longer!

> The greatest tragedy of life is not that men perish,
> but that they cease to love.
> — W. S. Maugham

And cease to write!

Heloise!

Where the hell are you!

> Being deeply loved by someone gives you strength;
> Loving someone deeply gives you courage.
> — Lao Tzu

> *Love makes the time pass. Time makes love pass.*
> — *French proverb*

Finally! But you are wrong ...

> Where there is great love there are always miracles.
> — W. Cather

> *Love ceases to be a pleasure, when it ceases to be a secret.*
> — *A. Behn*

H,

Now you know that isn't true! We hated the sneaking around. We wanted desperately to celebrate our love with everyone we knew. I remember you even cried once because I couldn't hold your hand in public ...

Ah, to touch that hand right now! It was like a small child's ... so helpless somehow.

Yes, you are truly the love of my life.

I see that now — so fully, and finally, and completely.

> Your Abelard

> *There are different kinds of love, but*
> *they have all the same aim: possession.*
> — *Roqueplan*

Heloise,

Yes, that much is true. Right or wrong — I want more than anything else in life to possess you!

  The desire for possession is insatiable.
  — A. Camus

Every man needs two women, a quiet home-maker,
and a thrilling nymph.
— I. Murdoch

You somehow managed to be both!

But if forced to pick, only a fool would choose the former.

Heloise,

No — I think you're wrong there. The world needs all kinds. Some people simply prefer peace and order to excitement and adventure. They prefer the familiar to the unknown — the safe to the risky. No need to judge them for that.

A

Trust me: those who play it safe have far more regrets in life.

As do the people who love them.

Oh, I have loved him too much to feel no hate for him.
— J. Racine

It is better to break one's heart than to do nothing with it.
— M. Kennedy

H,

All right, since you are tardy once again!

With love one can live even without happiness.
— F. Dostoyevsky

Yes ... how true ...

H,

Please take your turn now!

It's becoming increasingly difficult to find these.

    A

Heloise,

Where have you gone?

Isn't this one lovely!

> Soul meets soul on lover's lips.
> — P. B. Shelly

And in e-mail secrets . . .

H,

Please write me at once.

I'm beginning to get good and angry with you now.

Heloise,

Please find it in your heart to send me a few words.

I'm a pitiful sight waiting here all alone for your answer.

Your Abelard

H,

I suspect you're doing this to me on purpose! Are you?

All right, then, I'll share another happy memory with you now.

Of course you remember what we always did on New Year's Eve at precisely the stroke of midnight! ... ah, what happiness ... and we became quite expert at the timing of it all, didn't we ... ?

Your Abelard

A,

I've thought about you every New Year's Eve since the day we parted.

How could I not?

But those are the memories that keep me awake at night ...

In fact, only Dinah has given me any semblance of comfort at this time.

Yet how naïve our old favorites seem to me now. So ridiculously innocent and hopeful somehow ...

It is her quiet songs that speak to me now — the sad ones I never even noticed before.

From romance in the dark — to am I blue.

From sunny side of the street — to do you really want it that way.

From I'm in heaven tonight — to you let my love grow cold.

From if I had you — to a mean old man's world.

From let's fall in love — to trouble in the lowlands …

Oh, yes, I'd be singing entirely different songs to you now …

But there is one, and one alone, that I will never listen to again.

Invitation.

Never, ever again.

    Heloise

Dear Heloise,

Please tell me what other songs resonate with you now. I'll listen to every one of them — I promise. I need to hear them now …

On another subject, if I'm suddenly unable to write you for a short while (a small family matter) — please don't be alarmed. Just understand that I do, in fact, wish to contact you, but am simply unable to.

Never — ever — think that I've forgotten about you.

    Your Abelard

A

ctually I recall that you forgot about me for twenty-two long years.

And now you may go away for a while?

Suddenly my anger has returned in full.

Apparently you have understood nothing — nothing at all — about the depths of my despair at your very own hand.

Go away from me now.

And stay away forever.

Sweet Heloise,

How very wrong you are. Believe me — I do know the depth of your pain — intimately — deep in the gut — for it is also mine.

And I would gladly take on every bit of your suffering if I could — one hundred fold in fact. I would do almost anything for you now ...

You see, my entire being is crying out to possess you once again — for I did possess you at one time. I did. Just as you possessed me!

But what am I to do about it now ...

    Abelard

I simply wanted you to have the courage to love me — and the desire to fight for me.

Apparently it was too much to ask.

As for now, I simply want a final explanation about something suspicious in our past.

You cannot change a thing — now or ever — but perhaps you can explain certain disturbing things to me before we part once again forever.

H,

Are you saying you wish to revisit that place of great pain?

If so, then I must obey — but, personally, I think we have very little to gain.

A

Yes, revisit that place — if you dare.

Heloise,

All right ...

If you're sure ... yes, there was one more important similarity I conveniently failed to mention earlier on. Oh my goodness, this is difficult to write about ... Even now my heart is racing as I think back to that time ...

But yes ... you, too, got pregnant out of wedlock with your professor lover while still just a student ...

But there our story takes a much more tragic turn ...

And, yes — I'm the only one responsible for the most unhappy ending ...

You see, your pregnancy did scare the hell out of me — to the very core of my being. After all — neither of us wanted to have children ever — let alone at that tender age! We both knew — both of us, remember — that having a child was the absolute wrong decision for us. In fact we discussed all of this together at great length (surely you remember that). We very clearly discussed the fact that having a child was a good choice for many people — or even most — but not, I repeat, for us.

At that time, you may also recall, we cared only about loving each other. And after that we cared only about adding to the world scholarship of both art and history. It was a lofty ambition, wasn't it, that dream we both shared! We were going to write great books that people would talk about forever — which you may have done, by the way. So there is my proof, in fact. You were able to concentrate on your work. Except that we were supposed to make that contribution together ...

So if your question is why did I wish to terminate the pregnancy, then now you have your answer. Very simply, I was trying to protect us both from a lifestyle that just didn't suit us — particularly you who had so much talent to offer the world at large.

On the other hand, now, of course, I see that our child could have been our greatest contribution of all. Yes — most definitely. But how could I know that at such a tender age! I may have been older than you, my sweet, but I was still a very young man nonetheless.

I hope that my lengthy answers have satisfied you somewhat. I'm a very slow typist, you know, so this does take some time. (In other words, please read it all once again.)

    Your Abelard

Even at that young age — I knew what we were doing to our child.

I knew exactly.

Why didn't you?

H,

Yes, you did see the situation far more clearly than I at the time — I agree. And, yes, you did beg me endlessly to keep the baby — I know. In fact, I remember so clearly the image of you sitting at my feet weeping and pleading with me … yet I wouldn't budge at all you may recall. Oh, yes, I remember it all too well …

On the other hand, I did make it perfectly clear to you the final decision would be yours and yours alone. Please tell me you remember that part! And yet, as you say, words are cheap, for I did badger you mercilessly — in both subtle ways and not — to simply put an end to our problem and go through with the procedure … which, of course, you did.

Please forgive me for that!

Yes, indeed — I was a coward, wasn't I?

How could you even love a man such as myself!

A

What you call our problem was a human being.

And she would be 24 years old today.

She was my only chance at having a baby — or a little girl — or a grown-up daughter with children of her own.

Yet look what we did to her!

The procedure — as you call it — is by far the greatest regret of my life.

It was the worst decision of my life.

It was the most shocking, shameful, tragic event of my life.

It was both of us at our very worst.

I remain deeply, deeply ashamed of such a decision ....

Sweet Heloise,

I repeat … you are indeed a better person than I. But I've known that all along. Yes, she was our very own daughter … our very own … I remember the day we found out she was a girl. I was quite upset to learn that fact, by the way, though I hid it from you well. You see, that was the beginning of my own serious regret over the whole matter — for I was supposed to be her protector — not her killer!

Yes, even then I could see the tragic role I was playing in that terrible story …

Remember the letter H sent A after his castration? It could apply to you here as well.

> 'It was then that you alone paid the penalty in your body for a sin
> we had both committed. You alone were punished though we were
> both to blame, and you paid all, though you had deserved less …'

Once again, I apologize with every part of my being.

Abelard

Yet even after we learned that she was a little girl — even after we named her Anna after my mother (at your suggestion, you may recall) — even then you insisted on the test.

You needed absolute perfection — as if some flaw in her would make us love her any less.

In fact, it was quite the opposite.

I would have loved her all the more for it.

Heloise,

> The heart has reasons that reason does not understand.
> — Bossuet

Yes, I did insist on the test. But how could we possibly care for a disabled child? What did we know about that! You were still just a child yourself. I shouldn't have even been sleeping with you. And then to get you pregnant … I simply couldn't burden you with a baby at that young age. I simply couldn't. That was my exact line of reasoning (yes, I know, burden is a poor word choice again — please forgive my awkward bumbling — I am trying).

Yes, you were quite young for the test — but you may recall the doctor telling us it was the young, untested mothers who were having those babies now!

Heloise, you may hate and berate me all you like for the irresponsible part I played in this sad tale — but I've already beaten you to it.

Your Abelard

And yet look at the burden I was given in return.

H,

Please use our names when you write in the future. The brevity of your letters is already disturbing enough without the further insult of omitting our names on every page. I get upset each and every time I read them. Also, please include a polite greeting and ending of some sort from now on as well — for that is how civilized people behave in this day and age.

Also, I wish to start using your real name immediately. I assume I've earned that right by now. You're being very silly about all this and I'm beginning to get angry. Please stop playing these games! It isn't like you at all. Continue to express your thoughts honestly — yes — but also be polite about it, for god's sake. No matter what you tell me, I promise to listen with a genuine humility and objectivity — but you must also be kind in return.

From H:

> 'Where there is passion and love there is always struggle and turmoil. Now I am tired. I cannot reply to you because you are taking sweet things as burdensome and in doing so you sadden my spirit. Farewell.'
>
> A

You may ask me for nothing — nothing at all — ever again.

The reasons are obvious.

And no — you may never use my real name again.

Ever.

I see that tomorrow is your birthday.

At one time I considered it to be my own as well.

Still no mention of the outcome, I see.

Heloise,

Must we go on discussing things we are so powerless to change!

And I thought you forgave me temporarily.

And must you keep me waiting for so long — eight days is like eighty years to me now. Why are you being so cruel to me — you who were always so kind to everyone in your life. You must write me immediately about anything at all — your revulsion for me, your love for me — but please send me anything but silence for your tiniest words are like oxygen to me now.

You see, your face is right there, so close to mine all the time … I feel your soft lips and moist breath and tongue resting against mine …

Yes — I am going mad thinking about you again. My mind is all but gone. I cannot put together a single rational thought. I'm now just a fragmented, broken version of my old self.

In fact, the only thing I even recognize in myself any longer is the undeniable desire to devour you.

And yet — in the midst of all this chaos — I am completely happy for the first time in decades precisely because I have found you again.

Your Abelard

Heloise,

Why is it that I continue to wait for you — and continue to harbor such high hopes for an intimate, productive reunion with you? Every morning I feel a fresh wave of optimism that I'll hear from you again that day — but then, every night, usually around midnight, after hearing nothing at all, I once again slink off to my bed a sad and beaten man …

All right ... the outcome ...

No, we didn't expect to hear such terrible news, did we? I remember the doctor couldn't reach you for days, so he called me instead with the awful report. You were still in class, so I walked over and told you myself ... Then we roamed all over the campus for hours on end in a strange sort of daze. I also remember being unable to return to your place for quite some time after that. I suppose I saw it as re-visiting the scene of the crime ...

But is there a specific question you have for me?

Your Abelard

H,

Yes, you have every reason to punish me — but must you really do so?

We could be clarifying things here. And speaking about our rare love for each other!

Heloise,

Why the silence!

You're hurting me deeply.

Answer immediately.

Heloise,

Are you all right? And are you receiving these?

I'm beginning to get worried now.

Please write me at once.

The outcome pleased you.

H,

Now that is untrue! I wait here for what seems like an eternity — and then receive only those four brutal words from you?

Yes, perhaps the test results did come as a relief to me — but isn't that a normal reaction for a man who loves a woman — or rather a mere girl — to want the best for her! Yes — I did think the test results made the decision all the easier for us — not the reverse — I admit it — but isn't that human nature? Should I lie about it instead!

Also, my friend, forgive me — but if you want to hear more of my thoughts, you really must start sharing more of your own.

I cannot read your mind, you know.

A

You call it the scene of the crime?

I ask you: What pleasure can be found in loving a perfect human being?

None at all.

She was our very own baby — fully formed and waving her tiny arms.

I felt her move.

I would have loved her had she been born headless and without limbs.

Heloise,

I'm so sorry for my lack of tact. I mean well, I really do, but you were always the superior writer. You must simply look beyond my stumbling words for the sentiments and motivations I'm attempting to explain ...

Also, I'm pleased to hear that you actually prefer a flawed, imperfect human being — for then you will find plenty to love about me.

I can only say that, once again, I'm terribly sorry for my poor judgment in the past — you whom I wanted only to love and protect! My counsel was damaging to you in every respect, it seems — and, worst of all, it was irreversible. Very simply, it appears that I have never once, even for a moment, considered your own wishes and feelings.

And yet I did want only the best for you. Of that you can be certain …

 Your Abelard

P.S. Remember when you once said I use too many commas? I think I needed all those above.

P.P.S. Also, in my defense, I did warn you time and again to question every single one of my stubborn opinions and positions! Surely you remember that.

Heloise,

Please don't do this to me …

Heloise!

Please!

… take pity on me …

What is it that H wrote?

 'My love is constant and unchangeable.'

Yes, even when you do this to me.

I have spread my dreams under your feet.
Tread softly because you tread on my dreams.
— W. B. Yeats

Heloise,

Look what your namesake wrote.

Please take note!

> 'I beg you, be fearful for me always, instead of feeling confidence in
> me, so that I may always find help in your solicitude ... do not feel
> so sure of me that you cease to help me ... Do not suppose me
> healthy and so withdraw the grace of your healing. Do not believe I
> want for nothing and delay helping me in my hour of need. Do not
> think me strong, lest I fall before you can sustain me ...'

Yes, I know, you could express the same sentiments to me.

Then you left me behind to bleed all alone.

H,

Finally!

But that isn't true at all. Reprimand me if you like, but please do stick to the facts.

Immediately after the procedure I did leave you at your mother's house — yes — but that was at your request alone — not mine. I wanted you to be with me. In fact, I asked you repeatedly to remain at school near me — but you refused.

It is true, however, that I could hardly look into your eyes at that time — to see you suffering so terribly in every way. And when I picked you up again two weeks later, you looked even worse. Your entire personality had vanished beneath your empty, white face. You were both dead and alive. And it wasn't until a full year or so later that you actually began to look like yourself again ...

That's how I remember it anyway, my friend.

On another important subject ... is it really true that you never married or had children because of my influence on you?

That piece of information has served to haunt me since you first mentioned it. Sadly, perhaps my advice to you was based on an irrational sexual jealousy ... that is very possible. In fact, it's probably even true ...

As A once wrote (a sentiment I can certainly understand):

> 'At the time I desired to keep you, whom I loved beyond measure for myself alone ...'

And yet look what I've done — married twice — but not once to you. I suppose you should add the words hypocrite and madman to my list of flaws as well.

And yet — if you will indulge me for a moment or two — perhaps we've stumbled upon a familiar flaw of yours as well …

I remember very clearly that you would often submit to the will of others far less bright and talented than yourself … In fact, you often put other people's wishes and needs well before your own. Why is that, I wonder?

For example, why would you trust my counsel over your own on such an important subject as whether or not to have children! You see, My Darling, you have always believed too much in the opinions of others, instead of believing in your own …

Yes, you underwent the procedure despite your very best judgment.

But why is that, I wonder …

    Your Abelard

Do not steer the conversation away from our victimized daughter and onto myself.

When you see such a sweet child on the street now — what is it you think?

Heloise,

I've never known you to be rude before, but your continued thrift with words and lack of salutations are beginning to thoroughly demoralize me somehow.

I cannot lie to you. When I see such a person on the street I feel both relieved and saddened. I always study the parents far more closely than the child, however, for I always consider them to be better people than I (and I'm still trying to figure out why).

But listen, My Friend, I feel an overwhelming desire to speak with you again. This form of communication is simply too limiting in every way. Would you be willing to consider a phone call with me? Please think about it ... though I do suspect the mere sound of your voice would cause me to break down and weep ...

And yet not only do I want to hear you speak — I want to hear you laugh and sing and watch you walk and sleep and eat breakfast and work in your garden and pet your little cat (I'll bet you still have one) — and read a good book all snuggled up on my lap.

In short, how I do miss you right now.

I'm all yours, you know, all yours alone, if the real truth be known ...

(But please don't tell anyone ...)

    Your Abelard

The operative word is alone — for you have indeed left me all alone.

Yet somehow every single cell in my body cries out for you still.

And I cannot ignore even one of them — let alone all of them.

They have banded together and conspired against me.

They, too, have betrayed me …

H,

Oh, no — you left me first. As I recall, you left the country quite voluntarily and with much certainty that it was the right thing to do.

Let us both be very clear on that point at least.

A

No, you left me after the death of our baby.

You left me all alone for more than a year to suffer on my own.

But it's too late to change anything now.

Just like the many P.S.'s in your letters — all your explanations are more than a little bit tardy …

H,

> It is impossible to love and be wise.
> — Francis Bacon

All right, I think I understand now … Do you mean that I abandoned you in an emotional sense (and yes, a physical one, too) for about a year after that time? Yes, I suppose I did. Quite frankly, I was afraid of defiling you once again. I didn't feel worthy of either loving or touching you after that terrible, prolonged episode — yet I continued to have this great lust for you raging around inside of me that shamed me to no end.

Also, remember — we had been so careful the first time. So I trusted nothing at all except abstinence and a clear conscience at that point.

But I do remember the very morning our moratorium on making love finally came to an end. You were in the shower (one of my favorite places to find you, by the way), and you were singing something by Dinah very softly under your breath.

In fact, the song was 'If I Could Be With You' — and that morning we did 'what we might' all right …

Your Abelard

P.S. It just occurred to me that I actually behaved as if I were castrated for that full year. How very odd. Also, do you remember how we used to call each other Mommy and Daddy before all that happened? Yes, the irony abounds …

Defile me once again?

Oh, no, the defiling came much later when I signed my name to the death document — and when you kissed me good bye at the door — and when I pulled on the cold gown — and when I placed my legs in the stirrups — and when I allowed the death doctor to cut out our only child.

That was when the true defiling took place.

Another woman may call that room whatever she likes — and in good conscience. To her it may indeed be a room that gave her life.

But to me it will always be the Room of Death.

H,

Please let us leave that sad time behind.

Please let us finally move on.

A

I'll let you decide.

But no glib explanation will ever answer the most important question of all.

Why didn't you choose me!

H,

> Faint heart never won fair lady.
> — (can't remember who said that)

I'm afraid I have no further reasons to give you at this time. I've shared them all with you.

Most of all, I was, very simply, a coward.

But now I need more guidance from you.

Please send me all of your remaining questions — important, concrete questions that you still wish to have answered. No topic is off limits, and I promise to answer every one of them as honestly as possible, no matter how flawed they may reveal me to be.

For you deserve that, and much more from me.

I also need your questions to be timely — for I may have to go away soon.

I'm afraid there's been an illness in my family.

But I will write soon.

Much love,

A

A,

But you musn't leave me just yet!

*Of course your family should come first — always — but not just yet
… please …*

Don't you see — my life means nothing to me now.

Oh—when will I learn to trust you no longer.

I am numb.

I may even be dying.

Only you matter to me.

A,

Are you there?

I'm getting frightened now.

It's been another two weeks.

Please tell me where you've gone.

Please write me at once.

 H

Dearest Abelard,

 My love's a noble madness.
 — John Dryden

I must hear from you today.

Now I fear for your very safety.

You would never leave me to suffer this way.

Where are you, Sweet Abelard?

Where are you, My Love!

My Darling,

Perhaps I'll simply write anyway …

For maybe you are somehow reading my letters.

By the way, I must tell you something now.

You call yourself an obscure historian?

Hardly.

Every student who took a class with you was in complete awe of you. Every woman wanted to sleep with you, and every man wanted to be you. (Didn't Heloise write something like that as well?)

You were — and are — the most profound thinker I have ever come across.

Every semester you turned lazy, spoiled children into disciplined, questioning historians in a matter of fifteen weeks.

You were a magician — a sorcerer — on the subject of mankind and his past — no matter what the era.

You changed lives daily just by being yourself and sharing your magnificent thoughts — and I will regret forever the hundreds of lectures of yours I have missed over the years …

   Your Heloise

My Darling,

Icco … I beg you …

Please write me today … just one more time — even if just to explain!

I've been reading over their sweet letters again …

From H:

> '*In my case, the pleasures of lovers which we shared have been too sweet — they can never displease me, and can scarcely be banished from my thoughts. Wherever I turn they are always there before my eyes, bringing with them awakened longings and fantasies which will not even let me sleep. Even during the celebration of the Mass, when our prayers should be purer, lewd visions of those pleasures take such a hold upon my unhappy soul that my thoughts are on their wantonness instead of on prayers.*
>
> *I should be groaning over the sins I have committed, but I can only sigh for what I have lost. Everything we did and also the times and places are stamped on my heart along with your image, so that I live through it all again with you. Even in sleep I know no respite. Sometimes my thoughts are betrayed in a movement of my body, or they break out in an unguarded word ... who is there to rescue me out of the body doomed to this death?'* ...

I do await word from you!

> *Your Heloise*

My Love … I am in agony here.

I don't even recognize myself any longer.

I am neither awake nor asleep.

Neither sane nor insane.

Neither dead nor alive.

Neither you, nor me.

Please talk to me.

Where have you gone, Love of my Life …

I'm 'lost in a world of make believe dreams …'

> *The heart that has truly loved never forgets.*
> *— Thomas Moore*

What did George Eliot say about love?

It will have the soul all to itself.

My Love,

I may be slowly dying …

> How alike are the groans of love to those of the dying.
> — M. Lowry

> Absence is to love what wind is to fire;
> it extinguishes the small, it inflames the great.
> — Bussy-Rabutin

My Love,

I will continue to write you anyway.

I will — you will see.

Yes, the wind is to blame for all this …

> When we lose the one we love, our bitterest tears are called
> forth by the memory of the hours when we loved not enough.
> — M. Maeterlinck

My Dearest Friend in the World,

Sometimes I close my eyes and whisper things aloud to you.

Do you hear them somehow?

Please tell me that you do.

I'm becoming as mad as a hatter, it seems.

Sometimes I even hear you call to me … what a gentle way you have of saying my name.

Yes — what we discussed all those years ago is true:

Love is based on admiration alone.

And I simply admire you.

> *We do not believe in rheumatism*
> *and true love until after the first attack.*
> *— M. von Ebner-Eschenbach*

My Darling,

Where are you ...

You are wrong not to tell me!

And now I have yet another similarity:

All four of us loved quotations.

How could we have missed that one before?

How very strange it all is ...

(Also, of course I agreed with your quotations all along ...)

But here's the one I've been looking for since we began.

(You may recall we read this together in that awful B&B in Maine the night we couldn't go to sleep)

> *... as in our will*
> *To love or not; in this we stand or fall.*
> *— John Milton*

My Darling, we did once stand so tall!

'I wanna be loved!'

My Sweet Abelard,

Have you ever noticed how tears like to cling to the skin? They don't want to drop off. Instead they prefer to slide slowly down the cheeks and neck, creeping leisurely past the ears in big thick wet drops, tickling everything on the way down until they finally burrow somewhere together in a small mushy mess …

I don't even realize I'm crying now until I'm almost through …

Time out for tears all right.

Just remembering what it could be like …

   Your Heloise

Dear Abelard,

You cannot be ill.

You simply cannot be.

Suddenly I keep imagining you in a hospital room surrounded by worried loved ones while your little boys play loudly in the hall just outside …

It is you, my Abelard, not someone else I see in that sick bed.

Why is that!

Why do I keep seeing that!

Please tell me I'm completely wrong.

To quote my namesake:

> 'You alone have the power to make me sad, to bring me happiness or comfort ...'

And of course you remember this letter:

> 'God knows I never sought anything in you except yourself; I wanted simply you, nothing of yours. I looked for no marriage-bond, no marriage portion, and it was not my own pleasures and wishes I sought to gratify, as you well know, but yours. The name of wife may seem more sacred or more binding, but sweeter for me will always be the word mistress, or, if you will permit me, that of concubine or whore.'

Yes — all I ever wanted in the entire world was to be your whore.

I'm waiting, my love ...

Even just turning my face in your direction makes me feel so much closer to you ...

My Darling,

I called the History Department today and was told that you've been out on medical leave for a full academic year.

I am in a state of shock and disbelief.

So my imaginings were correct.

If you are gravely ill — and have withheld that information from me — I will never recover from it.

It will mean that you have robbed us of our last words together.

It will mean that my life is over as well.

Don't you see — I should have been singing your praises here in these pages — not berating you so mercilessly.

For I love you, My Darling.

I love you.

I love you . . .

My Dear Friend in both Happiness and Sorrow,

You told me recently what you love most about me.

Now it is my turn.

This is what I admire most about you: Your Heart — Your Talent — and Your Mind (in that order).

Believe me, no man ever loved a woman better . . .

My Darling,

There is something I must tell you now — and it is very important:

I forgive you for whatever secrets you may have withheld from me in the past.

Don't be frightened or worried about such things.

I will always forgive you, for everything, always — and that is a promise.

Also, no more questions or vague accusations.

If you can join me again here we'll write only about our lives now — and about our most interesting thoughts.

We'll find a completely innocent way to continue loving each other right here in this place — and we'll do it without hurting anyone at all.

And I will be satisfied with that.

I promise you that.

Just come back to me now … please.

From H:

> *'…you have it in your power to remedy my grief,
> even if you cannot entirely remove it …'*

My Love,

Please be well! I've so much more to tell and ask you.

For example, did you know that you always existed somewhere far outside my world view?

There was the whole world — and then there was you.

You see, I always wanted freedom — but not from you.

And I wanted privacy — but not from you.

And I wanted distance — but not from you.

And I wanted solitude — but not from you.

Yes, there was the whole world ... and then there was You.

My Sweet,

> *There is a sacredness in tears. They are not the mark of weakness, but of power. They speak more eloquently than ten thousand tongues. They are messengers of overwhelming grief ... and unspeakable love.*
> *— Washington Irving*

I've become quite good at crying now, you know. Sometimes I just let the tears spill out without any fuss or expression on my face at all. And then other times I prefer to moan and groan and summon up every bit of cheap theatrics I can.

Also, strangely, my body gets either very cold or very warm.

I hope you aren't weeping as well — lost and forlorn as I am.

My Darling,

>Whoso loves, believes the impossible.
>— E. B. Browning

I haven't given up hope yet.

Nor will I ever give up.

I will simply wait.

>Your H

My Sweet,

>Hate leaves ugly scars, love leaves beautiful ones.
>— M. McLaughlin

I finally called your home today — only to hear a sweet-sounding woman's voice on your answering machine.

I left no message.

If you are gone, I am gone also.

Do you remember how Heloise predicted their sad future apart?

>'We shall both be destroyed. All that is left us is suffering
>
>as great as our love has been.'

Please — let us finally be different from our unlucky namesakes!

Dear _____,

I have heard many wonderful things about you over the years from my good friend and client, _____.

I only wish that my reason for contacting you now were a happier one.

But the enclosed letter will explain everything to you in full.

Please accept my most profound condolences, for I, too, cared deeply about the man — as I know he did for you.

Also, please feel free to call me should you have any questions or concerns regarding his final wishes and instructions.

If I may step out of my professional role for a moment, I'd like to say once again that this was a man who loved you very, very much.

Again, best wishes, and I'm so very sorry for your terrible loss.

Yours Sincerely,

_____

Council to _____.

My Darling Heloise,

> The madness of love is the greatest of human blessings.
> — Plato

Greetings my Companion in Life and in Love — and now even Death.

I have instructed my close friend and attorney to send you this letter upon my impending demise (yes, I'm afraid 'Graduation Day is almost here, My Love').

Please forgive me for withholding the fact that I was gravely ill from you during our most recent contact. But I trust your kind nature will allow me one more bumbling transgression.

Also, please don't despair over my abrupt departure. For I've lived a very good, satisfying life — particularly the moments spent at your loving side. However, I do wish that I could have seen your sweet face one last time — and held your little hand one last time … but such is our luck (or lack of it), I suppose.

But, yes, I knew all along that I was dying of a cancer very similar to the one Abelard probably suffered from — which I suppose we could have predicted as well.

Why didn't I share this news with you before? Because then you would have raced promptly to my side to save me — or at least to care for me — and I would have then abandoned everything in my life in order to be with you. I would have left my home, my wife, my friends, my work — everything but my boys — in order to lie in your sweet arms again …

You see, to satisfy my own desperate wants and desires for you, I would have had to betray everyone else who was important to me — and that was a situation I simply could not allow to happen.

I have something else important to tell you now as well. There is, indeed, another reason why I didn't go looking for you during those long, lost years … It was because I was hiding a terrible secret from you … a shameful secret I was terrified you would uncover were I to see you again.

And that secret is this:

Our baby was perfect.

Yes — I lied to you.

Our daughter was, in fact, a perfectly healthy baby girl with no abnormalities whatsoever.

Yet I told you otherwise. And I also instructed the doctor and nurses not to discuss the matter with you further because of your highly vulnerable state (yes, I remember very well my exact duplicitous words to them). In my defense, however, I hadn't planned on deceiving you that way. The words simply slipped out of my mouth — and then, as they say, the lie seemed to take on a life of its own …

Please forgive me for this last cruel act of manipulation towards you — you who deserved so much more from me. Of course I see the error of my ways now — but at the time it seemed to make such perfect sense. You see, I thought I was protecting you. I thought I was taking care of you! I was wrong, of course, but I can assure you of one thing: My motives were always completely pure. It was your interests — and your interests alone — that consumed me, however misguided my advice might have been.

If I may quote H a final time:

> 'Wholly guilty though I am, I am also, as you know, wholly innocent. It is not the deed but the intention of the doer which makes the crime, and justice should weigh not what was done but the spirit in which it was done.'

(Believe me, I realize the sentiment behind that statement is far too generous to apply to me, but you'll understand my point.)

Also, we can add another similarity to our list as well. Yes, Abelard was a few months younger than I at the time of his death — but only my recent contact with you has kept me alive past my last birthday. And should the coincidences continue to mount — you will live for another full 21 years after me — though please do take your time.

This, then, leads to my most important news of all.

You see, I do have a warm Invitation for you after all …

My Darling, will you please join me one day — upon your own sad death — in the crypt where I now lie — to share Eternity with me wrapped up tightly in my arms!

I am serious about this.

Please say yes to this most important request.

It will be just as the real A & H did.

The paperwork, along with my notarized signature, will be sent to you shortly by my attorney should you decide to accept this offer. You should also know that my wife is in full support of this idea as well. (Now do you see why I loved her?)

You see, I told her what I did to you so long ago — and she wept real tears of sorrow on your behalf. She understands the depth of my betrayal to you now that she has two beautiful sons of her own …

So please say yes … Believe me, having you at my side for all of Eternity is my single greatest wish as I write this final letter, just days or even hours away from the end. Yes — I do hope you'll consent.

And, of course, you remember what happened when they re-opened the real Abelard's crypt in order to place Heloise's limp body beside his:

> 'It is said that when she was lying in her last illness she gave instructions that when she was dead she should be laid in the tomb of her husband. And when her dead body was carried to the open tomb, her husband, who had died long before her, raised his arms to receive her, and so clasped her closely in his embrace.'

My Darling, I shall do the same for you.

For in my heart I always wanted to choose you.

And now I have finally done so.

Yes, I have chosen you — and only you — after all.

How happy that makes me . . .

Also, when that time comes — and you join me here in this place — we shall finally reside together under the same roof.

So what do you think of that!

I will be waiting . . .

For you, too, are my Only Love.

    Your Abelard

P.S. Was it really so long ago . . . or maybe just an hour or so ago . . .

P.P.S. I hope I didn't use too many commas.

My Dearest Abelard,

> *When love is not madness it is not love.*
> — *P. de Le Barca*

Perhaps if I imagine your sweet face when I press the word Send, this final letter will reach you somehow …

After all, if we are to respect the etiquette of letter writing as our namesakes so liked to do — you well know the inferior of the two correspondents should always write last out of respect for the other, thanking him or her for such kind time and attention.

So I am writing you now for that very purpose.

Thank you for everything, My Darling, both past and present …

As for your final confession to me, I have something of my own to add to that as well.

You see, I knew all along about your attempt to deceive me. Yes, I knew from the first moment you spoke just what you were planning for me. How could I not? I've always understood your motives and actions far better than you did yourself …

I suppose all through the years I was simply waiting and hoping for an apology from you — one I received in just the nick of time it seems.

Perhaps our luck is better than we once believed.

Also, I forgive you completely for everything — of course I do — because I fully recognize the Ethic of Intention behind your deception (as H would call it). I know that you meant only to love and protect me above all else …

I also know what a gentle human being you were deep inside. In fact, you were the most giving person I have ever met in my whole life.

Yes, you were very kind to me in every single way.

And you know what Stevenson wrote about that all-important virtue:

'The essence of love is kindness.'

In fact, that may be my favorite epigram of all.

Also, before I go, I have important news to share with you as well.

I have decided to adopt a little girl.

I've requested an older child — someone who has been alone for a very long time. And I've also asked for a girl named Anna, if possible — and guess what? They've found one. In fact, I'll be meeting with her tomorrow ...

I've considered adopting off and on for many years, but only now does the time seem just right somehow.

Also, rest assured, My Sweet Darling — she will be told everything there is to know about you. After all, it was you — and you, alone — who brought us together ...

And yes — of course I will lie at your side for all of Eternity when the time comes for me as well. In fact ...

I shall but love thee better after death.
— E. B. Browning

It will be just as you say.

In fact, I look forward to the day.

And at that time you may also use my real name.

> Love, like a river, will cut a new
> path whenever it meets an obstacle.
> — B. Middlemas

Let us certainly hope so.

Farewell, my Great — and Only — Love.

> Your Heloise

P.S. Your commas are just perfect now.

CPSIA information can be obtained at www.ICGtesting.com
Printed in the USA
LVOW082340080212

267770LV00006BA/1/P